Katie AND THE WATERLILY POND

JAMES MAYHEW

ORCHARD

For Sarah

(who once crossed this bridge)
With love

ORCHARD BOOKS

Carmelite House
50 Victoria Embankment
London EC4Y 0DZ

ISBN 978 1 40833 245 0

First published in 2010 by Orchard Books
First published in paperback in 2011
This edition published in 2015

A CIP catalogue record for this book is available from the British Library.

3 5 7 9 10 8 6 4

Printed in China

Orchard Books is an imprint of Hachette Children's Group
Part of The Watts Publishing Group Limited, an Hachette UK company.
www.hachette.co.uk

www.jamesmayhew.co.uk

Acknowledgements
In the Woods at Giverny: Blanche Hoschede at her easel with Suzanne Hoschede reading, 1887 (oil on canvas),
Monet, Claude (1840-1926) / Los Angeles County Museum of Art, CA, USA / Bridgeman Images. *Bathers at La
Grenouillere*, 1869 (oil on canvas), Monet, Claude (1840-1926) / National Gallery, London, UK / Bridgeman
Images. *The Rue Montorgueil, Paris, Celebration of June 30*, 1878 (oil on canvas), Monet, Claude (1840-1926) /
Musee d'Orsay, Paris, France / Bridgeman Images. *Path through the Poppies, Ile Saint-Martin, Vetheuil*, 1880 (oil on
canvas), Monet, Claude (1840-1926) / Metropolitan Museum of Art, New York, USA / Bridgeman Images. *Waterlily
Pond*, 1899 (oil on canvas), Monet, Claude (1840-1926) / National Gallery, London, UK / Bridgeman Images

KATIE AND GRANDMA WERE visiting the art gallery.
"Look, there's a competition," said Grandma. "What fun!
You have to paint a picture like Claude Monet, the famous artist."
"Can I have a go?" asked Katie. "I'm quite good at art!"
"There's not much time," said Grandma. "The judging is at
three o'clock today."

Katie and Grandma decided to visit the
Claude Monet exhibition for ideas but Grandma needed
a rest first, so Katie looked at the pictures by herself.
"I bet I could paint a picture like that," she said.
"If I just had some paints . . ."
"You can use mine," called a voice.

Katie looked around, but the gallery seemed empty.

"Over here, *ma chérie*!" said the voice.

It seemed to be coming from a picture called *In the Woods at Giverny*.

Katie saw that Grandma was snoozing, so she stepped through
the frame and into the painting!

"That's a lovely picture," Katie said
to the lady who was painting.
"My sister, Blanche, was taught
by Monet," said the lady reading
a book.
"Claude Monet? The famous
painter?" asked Katie.
"That's right," said Blanche.
"Would you like me to teach you?"

Blanche showed Katie how to
mix the paints on the palette,
how to use the different
brushes, and how to fold
up the easel. Then she gave
Katie some paper to paint on.

"Now you are ready," said
Blanche. "Off you go, and good
luck with the competition!"
"Thank you!" said Katie,
jumping back into the gallery
with the painting things.

Katie looked around for ideas. She saw a picture of
some boats on a river called *Bathers at La Grenouillère*.
"I could paint the view from a boat," said Katie,
scrambling in. "That would be fun!"

There were so many boats to choose from.
Katie clambered into one and decided to row down
the river a little way to look for the perfect view.

Soon Katie found just the right place and began painting. It was going very well . . . until Katie heard a strange gurgling noise.

"Oh no!" she yelled. "The boat is leaking!"

Katie tried to row back to the
riverbank, but it was too far.
"Over here!" shouted some
bathers on a jetty.
Katie managed to reach them
just before the boat sank.

Katie rescued her painting things,
but her picture had floated far away.
"Boats are too much bother,"
said Katie. "I'm going to try
something else."

Back in the gallery, Katie saw
a picture of a street filled with people
waving flags and cheering. It was called
The Rue Montorgueil, Paris.
Katie couldn't resist climbing inside.

Katie found herself on
the balcony of a grand hotel.
People were waving flags from
the windows, while down below
a brass band was playing.
"I'm going to paint the parade!"
said Katie.

Katie ran down some steps onto the street and started painting.
The brass band got closer and closer.

Ooom-pa-pa! Ooom-pa-pa! The band got louder and louder
as it marched straight towards her.

Suddenly, Katie's picture was caught on the end of a trombone! Then, it was flipped up into the air and . . .

CRASH! Her picture was smashed between two cymbals . . .

And, finally, before Katie could catch it, her picture disappeared into a tuba!

"Good grief!" said Katie, as the band marched off through the crowds. "I need to find a nice, quiet picture with no one in it." So, she ran back up the hotel steps and into the gallery.

Katie looked around and spotted a lovely painting called *Path Through the Poppies.*

"What could go wrong there?" she said, as she clambered through the frame.

Katie skipped through the field of poppies and started to paint. It was so peaceful listening to birdsong and the gentle mooing of a cow.

"Hmmm, it's rather a large cow . . . and it has very big horns . . . Hang on!" Katie gasped. "That's not a cow – it's a bull!"

Suddenly, she remembered she
was wearing a red coat.
"Bulls hate red!" she wailed.

The bull started chasing Katie,
snorting as he ran!

Katie took a flying leap and
jumped into the gallery.

"Phew!" said Katie.
She looked back to see her painting
stuck on one of the bull's horns!
"You can keep it!" she laughed.

But time was ticking by, and Katie saw
it was nearly three o'clock.
"I'll have one last try," she said.
The nearest Monet picture was called
The Waterlily Pond.
"Here goes!" said Katie, climbing inside.

Katie saw she was in a beautiful garden.

"No boats, no brass bands, no bulls.

Perfect!" said Katie.

"Ribbit," said a frog.

"Hello, Frog!" said Katie. "Keep still

and I'll put you in my painting."

Katie started painting but the frog leapt away across the lily pads, chasing a dragonfly. "Come back!" called Katie, trying to follow him.

But Katie couldn't move – her feet were stuck in the mud!
She fell down with a splat, and her picture fluttered into the pond.

"Oh, I give up," said Katie, picking up the pond-soaked picture. "Painting like Monet is just too hard!"

She gathered everything up and went back into the gallery,
where she returned the painting things to Blanche.

"*Ma chérie*!" said Blanche, holding up Katie's soggy picture.
"That is beautiful."
Katie saw that the paints had smudged together and
her picture did look good!
"I'm just in time for the competition!" said Katie.
"Thanks for the paints and the art lesson."

Katie dashed to where the judging was taking place.

"A waterlily pond!" exclaimed the judges when they
saw her picture. "It's just like Monet. You win first prize!"

They presented Katie with a lovely set of paints.

"Oh, thank you," said Katie. "I'll have lots of fun with these!"

"What a wonderful painting," said Grandma, when Katie
showed her the picture. "How did you do it?"
"Well, I had a sort of lesson," said Katie. "Would you
like me to teach you?"
"That would be nice," said Grandma,
"but let's go and have a piece of cake first."
And so they did.

Get creative with Katie!

Claude Monet loved to paint plants, trees and flowers.
He had a beautiful garden at Giverny in France,
and the waterlilies he painted, and even the bridge
over the pond, are still there to this day!

I've tried to create a picture of reflections in water, a bit
like Monet's paintings. First of all I folded my paper in half.
On the top half I used very wet paint to make a picture
of a garden with a bridge. While the paint was still wet,
I folded the top half over the bottom of the page and
pressed them together. When I opened up the picture, it
looked like a reflection in a pond! It was great fun,
why don't you have a go?

Love Katie x